PUFFIN BOOKS

OF AN

HI I'M ROWLEY JEFFERSON.

HERE ARE SOME BOOKS MY BEST FRIEND GREG HEFFLEY WROTE.

THE DIARY OF A WIMPY KID SERIES

ALSO BY ROWLEY JEFFERSON

YEAH AND THEN YOU TOTALLY STOLE MY IDEA!

DIARY OF AN

Awesome Friendly Kid

I WROTE THE WORDS AND DREW THE PICTURES ALL BY MYSELF WITHOUT ANY HELP FROM A GROWN-UP!

Rowley Jefferson's JOURNAL

by Jeff Kinney

OK THEN WHO'S THIS GUY?

PUFFIN

PUFFIN BOOKS

UK | USA | Canada | Ireland | Australia
India | New Zealand | South Africa

Puffin Books is part of the Penguin Random House group of companies whose
addresses can be found at global.penguinrandomhouse.com.

www.penguin.co.uk   www.puffin.co.uk   www.ladybird.co.uk

First published in the USA in the English language in 2019
by Amulet Books, an imprint of ABRAMS
(All rights reserved in all countries by Harry N. Abrams, Inc.)
Published simultaneously in Great Britain by Puffin Books 2019
This edition published 2020

001

Cover design by Jeff Kinney, Lora Grisafi and Chad W. Beckerman
Book design by Jeff Kinney

Printed and bound in Great Britain by Clays Ltd, Elcograf S.p.A

A CIP catalogue record for this book is available from the British Library

ISBN: 978-0-241-40570-3

All correspondence to:
Puffin Books, Penguin Random House Children's
One Embassy Gardens, 8 Viaduct Gardens
London SW11 7BW

HERE'S SOME
BORING STUFF
THEY MADE ME
PUT IN HERE.

<u>My First Entry</u>
Hi I'm Rowley Jefferson and this is my diary. I hope you like it so far.

I decided to start a journal because my best friend Greg Heffley has one and we usually do the same stuff. Oh yeah I should mention that me and Greg are

I'm sure you're probably like "Well tell me more about this Greg guy." But my book isn't about HIM, it's about ME.

The reason I called my book "Diary of an Awesome Friendly Kid" is because that's what my dad is always saying about me.

ROWLEY YOU ARE AN AWESOME FRIENDLY KID.

Like I mentioned already, Greg is my best friend which makes my dad my SECOND best friend. But I don't tell him that because I don't want to hurt his feelings.

WE ARE BEST FRIENDS RIGHT SON?

PAT PAT

GULP.

Now that I brought up my dad I should
mention he doesn't seem to like Greg
all that much. And the reason I get
that feeling is because my dad is always
saying it.

I DO NOT
LIKE GREG.

But that's only because my dad doesn't
really get Greg's sense of humour.

Right now you're probably thinking "Hey Rowley I thought this book was supposed to be about YOU." Well you're right so from now on I promise there's gonna be a lot more Rowley in here.

The first thing you need to know about me is that I live with my mom and dad in a house at the top of Surrey Street, which is the same street my best friend Greg lives on.

I already talked about my dad but my mom is pretty great too because she feeds me healthy food and helps me keep my body clean.

SCRUB
SCRUB

Every morning I walk to school with my friend Greg. We usually have a total blast when we're together but sometimes I do things that annoy him.

But what REALLY gets on Greg's nerves is when I copy him. So I'm probably not gonna let him know about this journal because it's just gonna make him mad.

Anyway writing in this book is a lot of work so that's all I'm gonna do for today. But tomorrow I'll put a little more Greg in here because like I said we're best friends.

My Second Entry

OK so bad news: Greg found out about
my diary.

I guess I felt kind of proud that I had my
own journal and I wanted to show him.
But just like I predicted it made him MAD.

Greg said I totally ripped him off and
that he was gonna sue me for stealing
his idea. I said well go ahead and TRY
because you're not the FIRST person to
write in a diary.

Then Greg said it's a JOURNAL not a diary and then he whapped me with my own book.

WHAP

I told Greg if he was gonna be a jerk then I wouldn't say nice things about him in my journal. Then I showed him what I wrote so far.

At first he seemed annoyed because I always forget to draw noses on people. But then he said my book gave him an IDEA.

Greg said one day he's gonna be rich and famous and everyone will want to know his whole life's story. And he said I could be the one to WRITE it.

I said I thought that's what your
JOURNAL is for and he said that's his
AUTObiography but my book could be
his BIOGRAPHY.

Greg said there are gonna be a LOT of
biographies about him one day but he'd
give me the chance to write the first one.

I thought that sounded like a good idea
because I'm Greg's best friend and no one
knows him better than ME.

So I'm gonna start this book again with a
new title and now the main character is
gonna be Greg instead of me. But don't
worry I'm still gonna be in it a lot too.

DIARY

OF GREG

HEFFLEY

by Greg Heffley's
Best Friend

Rowley Jefferson →

EARLY LIFE

Most biographies about presidents and famous people start with a chapter called "Early Life". Well the problem is that I didn't meet Greg until the fourth grade so I don't know a lot about what happened to him before then.

I've seen a few photos hanging on the walls in Greg's house and from what I can tell he was a regular baby. And if he did anything important when he was little you can't really tell from the pictures.

Anyway fast-forward to right before
the start of fourth grade and now this
biography is gonna get a lot more detailed.

We used to live in a whole different state
but then my dad got a job and we had to
move. My family bought a new house at
the top of Surrey Street and we moved
in over the summer.

The first few days I didn't leave the
house because I was scared about being in
a new place.

I know you are probably wondering "Well
when is he going to meet Greg?" but just
wait because I am getting to that part.

My mom said maybe I should try to make some friends and she even bought me a book called "How to Make Friends in New Places" to help me do it.

The book had all kinds of things like knock-knock jokes to help a kid like me meet new people. But the tricks in the book didn't really work on Greg.

Luckily me and Greg became friends anyway.

I told Greg I lived in the new house at the top of the hill and he said that was kind of bad news for me because when our lot was empty he planted a flag there so now he owned my house plus everything in it.

But later on my dad told me that wasn't true and then he went to Greg's house to get my bike back.

I'm pretty sure that's the first time my dad told me what he thought about Greg.

I DO NOT LIKE GREG.

But I like Greg a LOT. He is always doing hilarious things like making me laugh right after I take a big gulp of milk.

BWAHAHAHA!

Plus Greg is always playing wacky pranks on me and they usually make me laugh pretty hard too.

So I'll bet you can tell why me and Greg have been best friends since fourth grade. I even got us a locket to make it official but Greg says those things are for girls and that's why he won't wear his half.

BEST
FRIENDS

Well I could probably fill up a whole book with all the zany things me and Greg do but since this is his biography I should probably write some stuff about his family.

Greg has a mom and dad just like I do but they are pretty regular parents so I don't have a lot to say about them.

But Greg isn't an only child like me. He's got an older brother named Rodrick who has a rock band called Loded Diper.

Some of their songs have swears in them so my mom and dad won't let me be at the Heffleys' house when Rodrick has practice.

Greg also has a little brother named Manny who is only three. And don't ask me why but the first time I went to Greg's for a playdate Manny randomly pulled down his pants and showed me his bum.

Now every time I see Manny he acts like we have this big secret or something which makes me feel uncomfortable.

Anyway I guess that wraps up the first chapter of Greg's biography. And if you're thinking "Rowley when are we gonna get to the exciting parts?" then just WAIT.

THE TIME I HAD MY FIRST SLEEPOVER AT GREG'S

After me and Greg met we had a few playdates at MY house and a few playdates at HIS house. Oh yeah I forgot, Greg doesn't like it when I call them "playdates" so I will have to change that in the next draft or else I'm gonna get whapped again.

Anyway me and Greg "hung out" a lot at each other's houses but then one day he invited me to his house for a SLEEPOVER.

I was pretty worried because I'd never slept away from home before. In fact I wasn't even sleeping in my OWN bed yet because I was scared.

I told my mom I was too nervous to stay at Greg's but I got a little LESS nervous when she said I could take Carrots with me.

When I got to Greg's we played in his room for a while but at 9:00 Mrs Heffley said it was time to go to bed. And she said we had to sleep in the BASEMENT. Well now I was SUPER nervous because I think basements are really creepy.

As soon as Mrs Heffley turned the
lights off, Greg said he needed to tell me
something important. He told me there's
a half man, half goat that lives in the
woods in our neighbourhood so I probably
shouldn't go outside alone at night.

Well I was NOT happy to hear that news
and I really wished someone told my
parents about this goat guy before we
moved into the neighbourhood.

Anyway the goat thing got me TOTALLY
spooked so I hid under the covers. But
I think Greg got pretty spooked too
because he crawled under them WITH me.

Then all of a sudden there was this crazy noise right outside the window and it sounded exactly how a half man, half goat would sound.

Me and Greg didn't wanna get eaten by this goat guy so we got out of there as fast as we could.

21

But we almost died anyway because we trampled each other running up the stairs.

We locked ourselves in the laundry room so the goat man couldn't get us. But that's when we found out it wasn't the goat guy at ALL, it was just Greg's brother Rodrick playing a trick on us.

OK this next part is embarrassing but since it's a biography I've gotta tell the whole truth. I wet my pants when we were in the basement and heard those noises outside.

Mrs Heffley gave me an extra pair of Greg's underwear but they were too small. So my dad had to come get me and bring me home in the middle of the night.

It was a long time before I was allowed to go to Greg's for another sleepover, but that's a MUCH longer story and I'm not even sure there's room for that one in this book.

THE TIME I SAVED GREG FROM TEVIN LARKIN'S BIRTHDAY PARTY

There is a kid named Tevin Larkin who lives over on Speen Street and last summer his mom invited me and Greg to Tevin's birthday party. We didn't wanna go because Tevin is hyper but both our moms said we HAD to.

It turned out that me and Greg were the ONLY kids invited to Tevin's party but we didn't know that until we got there.

After we gave Tevin his presents his mom said it was time for party activities.

The first activity was to watch this movie
about a guy who could turn into a bear and
an eagle and a bunch of other animals.

When the movie was over Tevin wanted
to watch it AGAIN. But me and Greg told
Tevin's mom we didn't wanna watch the
movie a second time so she said we could
move on to the other activities like pin
the tail on the donkey.

Well that just made Tevin MAD.

He got all wound up and started acting like the guy in the movie who could turn into animals.

I guess Tevin's mom was used to this sort of thing but me and Greg didn't know what we were supposed to do. We asked Mrs Larkin if she could take us home but she said there were still two hours to go in the party.

So we went out of the back door and waited in the yard for Tevin to calm down.

But eventually Tevin found us and now he was acting TOTALLY nuts.

I took a few steps back to get out of Tevin's way but that's when I fell into a giant ditch. Luckily the ditch wasn't TOO deep or I probably would've broke some bones. But when I got to my feet I heard this buzzing noise all around me.

It turned out there was a HORNETS' NEST at the bottom of the ditch and they were all stirred up.

I got stung twelve times and two of the stings were inside my MOUTH.

BZZZZZZZZ

Mrs Larkin drove me home early and Greg hitched a ride too.

Anyway Greg is always saying he "owes me" for getting him out of that party and I put it in this book in case I ever need to remind him.

GREG'S ACCOMPLISHMENTS

Every biography I've ever read for school has a chapter called "Accomplishments" so I figure I'd better add that in here before I forget.

The problem is that Greg is only a kid and most of his accomplishments haven't happened yet. So I'll leave some blank space here and I can fill it in later on.

1.
2.
3.
4.
5.
6.
7.
8.
9.
10.

THE TIME ME AND GREG DISTURBED AN ANCIENT BURIAL GROUND

If you were spooked out by that goat man story from before then you might want to skip this one. OK if you are still reading, remember I warned you.

One time me and Greg were playing vikings and ninjas in the woods and then some teenagers came by and ruined our fun.

BUT THAT'S NOT EVEN THE SCARY PART YET so keep reading.

Me and Greg went further back in the
woods to get away from those teens.
Greg said we should build a fort so
if they came looking for us we could
protect ourselves.

So we spent the rest of the afternoon
making a fort out of sticks and logs.

Greg said we should put some rocks in our
fort in case things got REALLY bad, but
it was starting to get dark and there
weren't a lot of rocks lying around in the
woods anyway.

But then I tripped over something and guess what? It was a big ROCK.

I told Greg I thought I sprained my ankle but he was a lot more worried about that rock than my injury.

Greg said it wasn't a rock, it was a GRAVESTONE and we'd just disturbed an ANCIENT BURIAL GROUND.

I guess you already knew that was coming because it was in the title of this chapter. I'll probably change it later on so I don't give the surprise away.

Anyway me and Greg were TOTALLY spooked out by this ancient burial ground thing and by now it was REALLY dark out so we were extra scared. But Greg must've totally forgot about my ankle because he took off and I couldn't keep up.

ZOW

I kept waiting for Greg to come back but he never did.

Luckily my parents called Greg's house to ask where I was and that helped him remember I was still out there.

And just to show you what a great pal Greg is, he let my parents borrow his flashlight and pointed them in the right direction.

DRAG

AN EVEN MORE SCARY STORY

OK while I'm on the topic of scary stuff I want to share a story about something that happened a couple of years ago.

One time I was at my grandpa's log cabin with my dad for the weekend and we took a hike and I got kind of dirty. Well technically it's my DAD'S cabin now because my grandpa died the year before.

I called my grandpa "Bampy", and the reason I called him that is because when I was two I couldn't say "Grampa".

But when I got older and I COULD say
"Grampa", nobody would let me change it.
And when my grandpa got older it's the
only word he really said.

WE LOVE
YOU DAD.

BAMPY!

So anyway back to the story. After I got
dirty from that hike my dad said I had to
take a shower.

But Bampy's cabin is really old and it
doesn't HAVE a shower, it just has one
of those creepy old-fashioned tubs.

After I filled up the tub with water and got in, here's what happened NEXT. I heard footsteps coming down the hall and I thought it was my dad bringing me a towel or something.

Then the door opened real slow, but guess what? NO ONE WAS EVEN THERE.

CREAK

I jumped out of the tub and ran around the house looking everywhere for my dad.

And if you're thinking "Oh Rowley the door thing was your dad playing a trick on you," well guess what? It WASN'T.

My dad was getting some milk at the store and he didn't come back until like a half hour later.

I told my dad what happened with the door and he said it was probably just the "wind".

But I know what it was: the GHOST OF BAMPY.

BAMPY!

THE TIME GREG PLAYED A
HILARIOUS PRANK ON ME

OK I know the last chapter didn't have a lot of Greg in it but I wanted to mention that story real quick because the Bampy thing totally FREAKED ME OUT.

If you like scary stuff then you're in luck because this one is pretty scary too.

One day me and Greg were hanging out at my house and Greg told me he saw on the news that there was a burglar going around breaking into people's homes.

Then he said he had to go home for dinner, and once he left I started getting scared because my parents weren't around.

But here's the thing: I found out later that Greg just PRETENDED to leave. He shut the front door but then stayed inside my house.

He took off his shoes and walked up the stairs super quiet so I couldn't hear him.

Then he started stomping around real loud upstairs. At first I thought it was the ghost of Bampy all over again.

Then I realized it was probably that BURGLAR Greg told me about and I almost peed my pants for the second time in this biography.

I heard footsteps coming down the stairs and I ran into the garage to hide from the burglar.

It was PITCH BLACK in the garage but I didn't want to make a move until I was sure that guy was gone.

Then all of a sudden the door to the garage opened real slow and I knew the burglar was gonna get me if I didn't do something. So I whacked him in the face with my dad's tennis racket and made a run for it.

Then I ran out of the front door and went to Mrs Monroe's house next door to tell her to call the COPS.

But then Greg came out of my house and that's when I found out the whole thing was just one of his hilarious pranks.

Greg was mad at me for two whole weeks and he said I should've known from the way the footsteps sounded that it was HIM and not a burglar.

I guess he's got a pretty good point about that since he is always playing wacky pranks on me. So I feel kind of bad about whacking him with a tennis racket.

but not really

<u>ANOTHER TIME GREG</u>
<u>GOT MAD AT ME</u>

<u>OK that last story made me remember
another time Greg got mad at me.</u>

<u>Me and Greg were walking home from
school a few months ago and there were
slugs everywhere because it just rained
the night before. And whenever there
are slugs lying around, Greg chases me
with one.</u>

<u>I guess it's pretty funny if you think
about it but it's never that funny when
it's happening.</u>

Luckily I am really fast when someone
is chasing me with a slug so I got away
from Greg by climbing up on the big rock
in Mr Yee's front yard.

Greg tried to get me to climb down but I
stayed right where I was.

Greg tried to fling the slug at me but he
lost his balance and almost fell in a giant
puddle in front of the rock. He was stuck
and I felt bad for him because he is my
best friend after all.

I got down from the rock and tried to help Greg. He told me to pull him back up to his feet but I guess I heard him wrong.

I grabbed him BY his feet and that turned out to be a pretty dumb move.

SPLOOSH

I didn't know WHAT Greg was gonna do once he got out of that puddle but I didn't wanna stick around to find out. So I ran to my house and locked myself in my room and didn't come out until Greg got called home for dinner.

The next day Greg said he was gonna get me back when I "least expect it". I just hope Greg forgets because when it comes to paybacks he's got a good imagination.

THE TIME WHEN GREG CREATED A SPECIAL AWARD JUST FOR ME

OK the last two chapters were about times Greg got mad at me but this chapter is the total OPPOSITE.

This one's about the time when I did something Greg thought was really awesome so then he did something really awesome for ME.

Anyway this one Saturday last autumn me and Greg were supposed to hang out at my house but he said he couldn't because he had to clean his garage. Then he said if I came and helped him we'd be done TWICE as quick. But I said no thanks I'll wait.

Then Greg said if I helped him he'd give me HALF of his Halloween candy.

Well that was a really big deal to me because my parents went through all my candy on Halloween night and they barely let me keep ANYTHING.

THREE PIECES OF CANDY IS <u>PLENTY</u>, ROWLEY!

GROAN

But I knew Greg still had a TON of candy because his parents don't make him throw out ANYTHING. So I told him OK I'll be right over.

Cleaning Greg's garage was hard work and it took like three hours.

After we were done Greg said OK now let's go hang out at your place.

I said hey what about that CANDY and Greg said oh yeah I forgot. But I knew that was gonna happen because whenever Greg owes me stuff he forgets.

We went up to Greg's room and he got his bag of candy out of the wardrobe.

But when he emptied out the bag it was almost all WRAPPERS.

The only things LEFT were three gobstoppers and a little box of raisins. I told Greg he promised me a TON of candy and he said he only promised HALF. Then he said a deal's a deal and he gave me a gobstopper and the box of raisins.

I told Greg I was gonna tell his MOM. And then Greg got real worried because he said his mom would be mad at him if she found out he ate all his Halloween candy already.

Greg said he was gonna give me something WAY better than candy, and he got out a piece of paper and a pencil and started drawing at his desk.

When Greg was done he handed me the
piece of paper and here's what was on it.

Greg said Good Boy awards are SUPER
rare and you have to do something really
AWESOME to get one.

He said I was EXTRA lucky because this
was the first ever Good Boy award he'd
ever given out and it was gonna be worth
a lot of money.

Well I knew Greg was just trying to get out of giving me the candy he owed me so I tried to act like I thought this Good Boy award thing was dumb. But somehow Greg could tell I thought it was kind of COOL.

Well that was only the FIRST Good Boy award but I got a lot MORE. For the next few weeks Greg made me one every time I did something awesome for him.

After a while I had a TON of Good Boy awards. And I kept them in a binder in clear plastic sheets so they wouldn't get messed up.

But then I started to feel like maybe my Good Boy awards weren't that rare any more since I had so MANY of them. Plus Greg was making the new ones a lot quicker than he made that first one and they didn't seem all that special.

So one time when Greg called and asked me to come down and help him rake his yard I told him I couldn't because I had homework.

And Greg said that's too bad because he came up with a totally new kind of Good Boy award and he was sad I wasn't gonna get to see it.

I was like well at least TELL me about it, and Greg said he COULDN'T because it was top secret and he didn't wanna ruin the surprise.

Then he said he was gonna call Scotty Douglas and see if HE wanted to help rake the yard and I said OK I'll be right over.

Well I wish I knew we had to rake the front yard AND the back because it was a lot of work. Plus I had to do it MYSELF because Greg was busy making that new award.

When I was finally done Greg gave me my award and I've gotta say it was even more awesome than I THOUGHT it would be.

This new one was called a SUPER Good
Boy award. Greg said one Super Good Boy
award was worth FIFTY regular Good
Boy awards and I could totally see WHY.

In the next few weeks I earned a BUNCH
of Super Good Boy awards but after a
while even THOSE didn't seem all that
special.

Besides I was spending a lot of time doing
stuff for Greg and I wasn't getting my
OWN chores done.

But every time I told Greg I didn't need any more Good Boy awards he'd come up with something NEW and then I'd have to have THAT.

After a while I had so many awards that my binder was STUFFED and I couldn't fit new ones in. So I told Greg I wasn't gonna try to earn any more no matter WHAT.

But Greg said that's OK because he made up a whole NEW system and I should probably just recycle my old awards.

I was pretty mad because I worked HARD for those awards and now Greg said they were totally WORTHLESS.

But I was still curious about this new system so I asked him about it. Greg said the new idea was called "Li'l Goodies" and it was a POINTS system and there wasn't any paper involved.

Greg said that every time I did something NICE for him I'd get a Li'l Goodie point. And once I got fifty Li'l Goodies I'd get a Fantastic Prize.

I was like OK what's the prize? And Greg said he couldn't tell me but it was under a sheet in his bedroom.

Well I couldn't figure out what was under that sheet but I could GUESS. And a LOT of my guesses were things I really wanted.

So I spent about a month doing lots of things for Greg and he gave me a Li'l Goodie point each time, like he promised.

Eventually I got to fifty Li'l Goodies. And I told Greg I was ready to turn them in for that Fantastic Prize.

But Greg told me that since it was the first day of the month my Li'l Goodie total got reset back to ZERO. And I said well you never told me about that rule and he said well you never ASKED.

I was really MAD and I yanked the sheet off the Fantastic Prize so I could see what it was.

But guess what? It was a LAUNDRY BASKET filled with dirty clothes.

I told Greg he was a crummy friend for making me do all that work for a phoney prize. But he said the laundry thing was just a TEST to see if I'd peek and that I failed the test.

Then he said the REAL prize was locked in the basement and that now I was gonna have to earn a HUNDRED Li'l Goodies to get it.

All I can say is I'm not a FOOL. I'm gonna take my TIME earning those Li'l Goodies, so if Greg thinks I'm in a rush to get that Fantastic Prize he's gonna be disappointed.

THE TIME I FOUND OUT GREG IS A LOUSY STUDY PARTNER

OK I know this is Greg's official biography and I don't want to put any negative stuff about him in here. But Greg if you are reading this I just need to say you are a TERRIBLE study partner. I hope that doesn't hurt your feelings but somebody has to tell you the truth.

Most of the time I don't really need to study for tests because I pay attention in class and I do my homework. Plus Mom always says it's important to get a good night's sleep so on school nights I go to bed extra early.

But this one time we had a really hard chapter in maths and I had trouble paying attention in class that week. That's mostly because Greg moved to the seat right behind me.

The night before the test I knew I was gonna have to go over the chapter and do some practice problems at home. But when I told Greg my plan he said we should study TOGETHER.

I wasn't sure that was such a good idea because when it comes to school stuff sometimes it's hard for Greg to focus.

But Greg said we're best friends and best friends should study together so I guess that made sense to me.

Well the FIRST thing we had to do was find a place to study. Greg said we couldn't be at HIS house because his brother Rodrick was having band practice.

And Greg was banned from MY house because he played a practical joke where he put cling film over our toilet bowl and he got my dad pretty good.

Greg said we should go to the LIBRARY
because it was quiet there and nobody
would bug us. So Mrs Heffley gave us a
ride to the library after dinner and we
found a table where we could do our work.

We got out our books and I said maybe we
should do practice problems to see what
we needed to work on. But Greg said he
hadn't even READ the chapter yet so we
needed to start from the BEGINNING.

Well that was kind of a waste of time
for me so I told Greg he could read the
chapter on his OWN to catch up. But
Greg said I was being a bad study partner
and that we were supposed to do
everything TOGETHER.

I said OK fine let's start from the beginning of the chapter and go through the whole thing. But Greg said before we got started we needed to plan our study breaks so we didn't get too stressed out.

Then he said we should START with a break so we'd get off on the right foot. And that's what we did even though it seemed like a bad idea to me.

FLICK

After like ten minutes I said we need to get to work because it's a long chapter and we have a lot to go through.

Well don't ask me why but Greg pinched
his nose with his fingers and said the
exact same thing I said but with a really
annoying voice.

I told Greg to stop copying me but that
just made him copy me even MORE.

Finally I got smart and started reading
the chapter out loud.

ANGLES IN A
TRIANGLE ADD UP
TO 180 DEGREES.

ANGLES IN A
TRIANGLE ADD UP
TO 180 DEGREES.

A RIGHT ANGLE
IS 90 DEGREES.

A RIGHT ANGLE
IS 90 DEGREES.

After a while Greg figured out what I was
doing and he stopped copying me.

I told him maybe it would be better if we
both just read the chapter quietly, but
Greg said that wasn't his "learning style"
and he needed to make things FUN so
they would stick.

I said what do you mean? And Greg said he
knew a way to make learning maths into a
GAME.

First he balled up a piece of notebook paper. He said we should take turns reading a few words from the chapter and toss the paper ball back and forth each time. So we tried it and it worked for a little while, I guess.

But whenever someone DROPPED the paper ball Greg said we had to start the whole page AGAIN.

And sometimes I think Greg was trying to make me drop the ball on PURPOSE.

I told Greg we were wasting too much time and we needed to do this another way. And Greg said he didn't care HOW we studied as long as it was FUN.

So I told Greg a trick my dad taught ME. He said that whenever I had trouble remembering something I should make up a SONG to make it easier.

Then I sang the song I made up to help me remember how to get the area of a circle.

Greg said that was the dumbest thing he ever heard and I said well if it's so dumb then why do I have 95 in maths and you only have 72?

I guess Greg didn't have a good answer to that and he said it was time for another break. So we played video games on the library computer until some grown-up reported us to the librarian for making too much noise.

When we got back to the table Greg said
we weren't studying the right way and
that he had an idea of how we could do
it BETTER. He said he'd read the FIRST
half of the chapter and I'd read the
LAST half and then we could team up
during the test.

I said well you're not allowed to TALK
during the test so I didn't see how that
was gonna work. Then Greg told me
about these monks who can transmit
their thoughts through the air if they
concentrate real hard.

So we tried doing it but I guess I couldn't concentrate good enough to make it work.

Greg said we needed to figure out a DIFFERENT way to communicate during the test.

I said if we just studied the chapter we wouldn't NEED to communicate, but once Greg gets something in his head he doesn't let it go.

He made up this whole system of sneezes and coughs and stuff so we could talk to each other during the test without our teacher Ms Beck noticing. But there was a lot to remember so I wrote it all down.

I said well what if one of us needs to ask the other guy a QUESTION and Greg said you just put a question mark at the end. And I said well we don't have a signal for a question mark and Greg said it could be a fart.

I told Greg I didn't think I could fart if I didn't really NEED to and Greg told me to try anyway and I did but nothing came out.

So Greg told me some different foods I could eat for breakfast that would make it easier to do a question mark.

But that idea made me nervous because
the last time I went to Greg's we drank
a lot of soda and tried to burp the
alphabet, and I got sick on the letter "B"
and had to go home early.

Greg said OK if I couldn't fart for REAL
then it would be OK to make a fake fart
noise under my arm.

That's when I told Greg I thought this was a bad idea and it was CHEATING to send each other signals during the test.

Greg said I was being a goody-two-shoes and that the only reason I wanted to get a good grade in maths was because I was a teacher's pet and I was in love with Ms Beck.

I said I was NOT in love with Ms Beck but that I just like her personality and the way she smells.

So Greg said that PROVES I'm in love with Ms Beck and then he sang that song about two people sitting in a tree.

I knew Greg was trying to make me mad
but for some reason the song didn't really
bother me that much.

I guess Greg got mad that he wasn't
making ME mad so he started singing
even MORE.

I tried to tune him out but he just got louder and louder.

Then I went into the bathroom and tried to study in THERE but Greg followed me.

But I guess somebody else complained because the librarian came in and told us we both had to get out of there.

Then she said if we made any more noise she was gonna have to call our parents and have them come get us. Well that sounded great to ME but I don't think Greg was ready to go home so he promised we'd quieten down.

I really didn't wanna sit at the same table as Greg any more so I moved to one of those desks with dividers between them. But Greg sat right across from me.

I was starting to get some work done but then Greg slid a note under the divider.

He had a maths question so I answered him and passed the note back.

Hey Rowley what do the angles in a quadrilateral add up to?
-Greg

360 degrees.
-R

And then Greg asked me ANOTHER question. But I didn't really mind because this was a MILLION times better than the way we were doing things before.

But then Greg slid the note back and it had another question on it that didn't have anything to do with maths at ALL.

Check one. I am embarrassed I wet the bed last night.

☐ YES

☐ NO

Well I checked the NO box because I DIDN'T wet the bed. I slid the note to Greg but then he wrote something on it and slid it BACK.

☐ YES

☒ NO

Ha ha ha you're not embarrassed you wet the bed.

That made me kind of mad because that's not what I MEANT. But I didn't wanna spend a lot of time explaining myself because I really needed to get back to studying.

So Greg wrote ANOTHER note and slid it under the divider.

Truth or Dare?

☐ TRUTH   ☐ DARE

I didn't wanna take a dare from Greg so I picked TRUTH. But I didn't like the question Greg came up with.

☒ TRUTH   ☐ DARE

Are you in love
with Ms Beck?

OK I switch
to Dare.

Then Greg dared me to get him a drink
from the vending machine. I didn't know
that was the way truth or dare WORKED
but I was just glad Greg didn't make me
answer that question.

After I got Greg his drink I did a little more
studying but then he started up with the
notes again.

Well I didn't like THAT so I sent back a
drawing of my OWN.

And then Greg drew another picture of
ME and I drew another one of HIM.

After a while we filled up two whole
PAGES with drawings.

Greg tried to start a NEW page of drawings but I just ignored him. And I guess he didn't like that because he kept trying to get my attention.

I decided to move to a new spot that wasn't so close to Greg. I was glad I could finally get some peace and quiet but THAT didn't last long.

If you're wondering what that "bang" was all about, well here's what happened. When I got up and moved to another desk some grown-up took my spot. And I guess Greg thought it was still ME and he tied the guy's shoes together.

Then when the guy stood up he fell backwards.

BANG

After that happened Greg got out of there as fast as he could. I figured I'd better get out of there TOO because I didn't want that guy to think I was the one who tied his shoes together.

I followed Greg into the children's section where there was an empty table. He put his stuff at one end and I sat down at the other so I didn't have to be too close to him.

Greg said we should take another study break but I said I was gonna keep working. Then Greg balled up a piece of paper and tried to throw it in the trash can across the room.

He missed but he kept shooting balled-up pieces of paper which made it hard for me to concentrate.

Then Greg finally got one in and he said he bet I couldn't make the same shot as him. But when I told him I really needed to study he said I was too scared to try and then he started acting like a CHICKEN.

I tried to ignore him but it wasn't so easy, ESPECIALLY when he got up on the table.

BROCK BROCK
BROCK BROCK

Then all of a sudden Greg sat down on the table and started making grunting noises. At first I thought he might be having a bathroom emergency. But when he got up there was an EGG.

Well I didn't want Greg to lay another egg so I balled up a piece of paper and tossed it at the trash can. And I wasn't looking to see if it went in but I guess it DID.

Greg said my shot was total LUCK and there was no WAY I could make it again even if I tried a thousand times. But I decided I wasn't GONNA try again.

Greg said I COULDN'T retire but I said
yeah I COULD. And it was his own fault
for giving me the idea anyway.

One time I had my birthday party at the
bowling alley and Greg hit a strike with his
first ball. Then he retired and it ruined the
game for everyone else.

When Greg couldn't get me to UN-retire he
tried making a backwards shot HIMSELF.
But he went through like a million pieces
of notebook paper and he couldn't even
come CLOSE. I was just glad he was
leaving me alone because I was getting a
lot of work done.

I finished the practice test and then I was gonna go over my notes from class. But that's when I found out Greg was getting all his paper from MY NOTEBOOK.

Well that made me really mad because Ms Beck said we were allowed to look at our notes during the TEST.

So I got down on the floor and started picking up all the balled-up pieces of paper. I figured maybe I could smooth the pages out when I got home and then tape them back into my notebook.

But Greg just kept SHOOTING and he finally got one in by bouncing it off my HEAD.

Well that made me really mad and I started chasing Greg with that egg he laid.

But I guess we were making too much noise and that got us in trouble with the librarian again.

She made me call my parents to come get us and that was fine with ME.

I had to stay up for two more hours uncrinkling my notes and taping them into my notebook and was up ANOTHER half hour researching stuff on my dad's computer.

SEARCH [can people lay eggs]

THE TIME I MADE THE BIGGEST MISTAKE OF MY LIFE

OK this is just part two of that last chapter but I got so mad writing it I kind of had to take a break. But I've gotta take some deep breaths because this chapter is gonna be even HARDER to write.

The next day during the maths test I tried to use my notes to help but they were all out of order.

Plus it was hard to concentrate because Greg kept trying to ask me questions.

Some of the OTHER kids were getting
stressed out about the test too because
Timothy Lautner got dizzy and Ms Beck
had to take him to the nurse's office.

Well as soon as Ms Beck left the room
Greg scooted his chair real close to mine
and looked over my shoulder.

SCOOT
SCOOT

I whispered to Greg to go away because
he was trying to CHEAT. But Greg said
it's not cheating since we were study
partners and we both had the exact same
information in our brains.

I guess he had a point but I still didn't feel
GOOD about it.

Then Greg said he already FINISHED his test and was only trying to make sure I got the right answers. And that made me feel kind of nervous because I wasn't positive about a few of them.

So I let Greg check my test, and believe me if I could do everything over again I wouldn't have LET him.

YEP. I GOT "180" FOR NUMBER EIGHT TOO.

MM HMM. YEAH, THIS IS SOME REALLY GOOD STUFF.

After a minute I started thinking maybe Greg wasn't just looking over my test to check my answers but that he was COPYING me.

And it was too late to STOP him so I tried to pretend it wasn't happening.

Greg pushed his chair back to its normal spot right before Ms Beck came back. And when the bell rang for the end of class she went around and collected all our papers.

The next day Ms Beck gave us our tests back and I got 89. I was kind of disappointed in myself because I usually do a lot better. But Greg got 89 too which was a really good grade for HIM.

But if you think this chapter has a happy ending, well guess what? It DOESN'T.

When class ended everyone got up to leave but Ms Beck told me and Greg to stay in our seats.

After everyone left Ms Beck told us she wanted to talk to us about our tests. She said she noticed we got the same grade and we got the same answers right.

But Greg said that made SENSE because
we were study partners and we knew all
the same stuff.

I felt pretty glad Greg was my friend
because he's real good at explaining stuff
like that to grown-ups.

I thought Ms Beck was gonna let us
leave but she DIDN'T. She said it seemed
a little suspicious that our tests were
IDENTICAL and she put them side by side
to show us what she meant.

Well that's when I found out Greg copied
EVERYTHING on my test, even my
NAME.

MATHS 2   NAME: Rowley Jefferson

Chapter 8 Test   (89)

1. A point has no dimensions, only ~~position~~.

2. A polygon is a 2-dimensional shape made up of straight lines.

3. Angles in a triangle add up to 90 degrees.

4. The area of a circle is πr^2.

5. What kind of lines are these?
   parallel

Ms Beck said it was obvious that Greg
copied my paper so he was gonna have to
do three days of detention PLUS he had
to take the test again.

I thought Ms Beck was gonna give me
detention too but she DIDN'T. But what
she said was WORSE than detention.

ROWLEY I AM
DISAPPOINTED
IN YOU.

Ms Beck said she wanted us to learn a
lesson from this and we both swore it
would never happen again. Ms Beck said
well that's good because once people
know you're a CHEAT it follows you
wherever you go.

Then Ms Beck said we were free to go. Greg got up and left but I gave Ms Beck a hug to show her I was sorry. But I think maybe I hugged her for too long.

On the way home from school all I kept thinking about was what Ms Beck said about being a cheat.

Well I learned MY lesson but I'm not so sure about Greg.

The next day Ms Beck made Greg sit at the back of the class and retake the test. But Greg was asking me questions pretty much the whole time and I had to pretend I couldn't hear him.

And if you're like "Rowley why are you still friends with Greg?" well my answer is that Greg's still a good FRIEND, he's just a bad study partner.

Plus he's the only person I know who can lay an egg.

THE TIME GREG TOTALLY
HAD MY BACK

OK Greg if you're still reading this then sorry if I made you look bad in the last two chapters. But don't worry because in this one you're gonna come out looking pretty good.

So last year our science teacher was Mrs Modi, but when she had a baby the school got this guy named Mr Hardy to fill in for her.

I think Mr Hardy used to teach at the school a long time ago and now they bring him back whenever they need a long-term sub.

Mr
Hardy →

I thought Mr Hardy was just going to do things the same way as Mrs Modi but I was WRONG. All Mr Hardy did every day was write our assignment on the board and then read at his desk for the rest of class.

Assignment:
Do problems 1–11 on page 92.

After like the third day, kids started goofing off during class. And Mr Hardy didn't even CARE.

One time a couple of kids tried to kill a bug by dropping their textbooks on it. Luckily the bug got away but even with all the noise Mr Hardy never looked UP.

THUMP   WHOMP

Well maybe Mr Hardy wasn't bothered but I couldn't concentrate on my assignments with all that craziness going on every day.

Greg told me I was wasting my time doing the daily assignments because Mr Hardy was never gonna even LOOK at them. Greg said I should just live it up with everyone ELSE until Mrs Modi returned and things went back to normal.

Well guess what? Mrs Modi DIDN'T come back. She decided she wanted to be a full-time mom and that meant Mr Hardy was our teacher for the rest of the YEAR.

Now that Mr Hardy was our official science teacher I thought things would get better. But they got WORSE.

Then on the last day of school Mr Hardy announced he was gonna give everyone their GRADES. Well that freaked out most of the kids in my class because just about everyone in there deserved an "F".

Mr Hardy started going down the aisles and whispering each kid's grade in their ear. But Mr Hardy doesn't have a whispering voice so everybody else could hear what he was saying.

The first kid to get his grade was Dennis Diterlizzi and he got a "C". But Mr Hardy talks real slow so it sounded more like this:

The next kid got a "C" too and so did
every kid after that. Even Greg got a "C"
and he didn't hand in a single assignment.
And he was real happy about it because
he didn't wanna go to summer school.

So then it was MY turn and I was kind
of crossing my fingers hoping I'd get a
GOOD grade. But I got the same grade as
everyone ELSE.

So I guess Greg was right that Mr Hardy never looked at those assignments.

Mr Hardy moved on to the next kid but all of a sudden Greg stood up and argued with Mr Hardy. Greg told him I was the only kid who did any work and that he's a terrible teacher and that someone should report him to the PRINCIPAL.

I was pretty shocked because Greg never stood up for me like that before. For a second I thought Mr Hardy was gonna send GREG to the principal.

But after a minute Mr Hardy whispered the NEW grade in my ear.

On the walk home I told Greg he was a great pal for doing that for me. And I said now we were even for that time I saved him from Tevin Larkin's birthday party.

But Greg said what he did for me was WAY better than getting him out of Tevin's party. He said by getting me that "B" he probably just saved me from getting some crummy job later on in life.

So I said OK how much more do I have to do until we're EVEN? And then he drew a chart to show me.

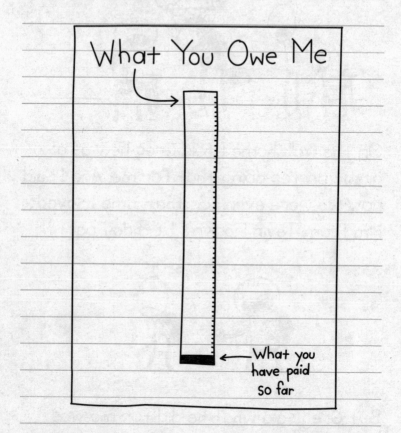

What You Owe Me

← What you have paid so far

I guess that means I've got a long way to go. But that's OK because me and Greg are gonna be friends for a long time and I'll get a lot of chances to pay him back.

THE TIME I REALIZED MAYBE GREG
DOESN'T ALWAYS TELL THE TRUTH

So after that time me and Greg were
study partners I asked him how the heck
he laid that egg and he told me he can lay
any kind of egg he WANTS.

And I said OK then lay an OSTRICH egg,
and he said for that he'd need to eat
a lot of crisps and then he took some
of mine.

But a few days later when I stopped by
Greg's house to pick him up for school
his mom gave him an egg for his lunch.
And then I remembered Greg ALWAYS
has a hard-boiled egg for lunch and so he
must've had one in his coat pocket the
night we studied together.

Well that made me start to wonder if some OTHER stuff I know about Greg isn't true. We've been friends a long time and he's told me a BUNCH of things that seemed a little shaky so now I'm kind of thinking not everything he's told me is a hundred per cent accurate.

Here are a few things I'm starting to wonder about.

1. Greg says he is dating a supermodel but they have to keep it a secret since her career would get ruined if people found out she was dating a middle-school kid.

Greg said whenever she goes on TV she sends him secret messages by blinking.

2. Greg says that one time he threw a frisbee and the wind took it so far that it went all the way around the world and hit him in the back of the head so that's why he won't play sports any more.

3. Greg says that the "star" on the keypad of a phone is really a SNOWFLAKE and it's a direct line to the North Pole. So whenever I do something Greg doesn't like he tells me he's gonna report me to Santa.

4. Greg says that when he was a baby his mom brought him to a modelling agency and they took some pictures for diaper cream ads.

Greg said the ads never ran in the United States but that if he went to China he'd get totally MOBBED.

5. Greg says that he came up with the "DE-FENCE" chant at basketball games and every time a crowd says it he gets one hundred dollars sent to his bank account.

6. Greg says he's 500 years old but he doesn't age and he has to move every few years so no one will figure it out. He says he knew Abraham Lincoln in middle school and he was kind of a jerk.

7. Greg says there's a form you can fill in at the town hall to legally adopt any kid you want, and that he adopted me so now I have to do whatever he tells me.

8. Greg says that he can turn into any form of water whenever he wants, but when I asked him to turn into a glass of water he said the LAST time he did that Rodrick drank him and it took two days to get back to human form.

9. Greg says he only uses five per cent of his brain, and if he WANTED to he could levitate a building with his mind. I said maybe I could levitate a building too but he said probably not because I'm already using one hundred per cent of my brain.

10. Speaking of BRAINS, Greg says he's got ESP and he always knows what I'm gonna do before I do it.

That one might actually be true because I've seen him do it a bunch of times.

Anyway I'm guessing at least HALF this stuff is made up but I'm just writing it down here in case it ISN'T.

And for the record Greg's been eating a LOT of my crisps over the last three weeks and there's still no ostrich egg.

THE TIME ME AND GREG CAME UP
WITH OUR OWN SUPERHERO

OK this is probably gonna be the best
chapter in this book because it's the only
one that's got superheroes in it. And I
hope I didn't spoil the surprise but even if
I did, trust me it's still gonna be a pretty
good chapter.

This one day it was raining so me and
Greg couldn't go outside. And Greg wasn't
allowed to play video games because he
lost his temper playing Twisted Wizard.

Mrs Heffley said kids our age spend too much time in front of screens anyway and it was good for us to take a break.

Then she gave us some markers and a sketchbook and told us we should use our imaginations and make up our own comics like we USED to.

Well the LAST time me and Greg made some comics together it didn't turn out so good for me. And if you don't know the whole story then I'll give you the short version.

In our first year of middle school me and Greg worked on a comic together called "Zoo-Wee Mama".

But then Greg got bored of it and said I should do it by MYSELF.

And then my comic got in the school paper and Greg was mad at me even though he's the one who TOLD me I should do it.

Then we got in a big fight in front of the whole school and some teenagers came out of NOWHERE and they caught me and Greg.

Then they made me eat a piece of _____ that was on the basketball court.

I still can't eat pizza or mozzarella sticks or anything else with _____ in it but Greg says I need to "get over it" because that happened a long time ago.

So anyway when I opened that sketchbook Mrs Heffley gave us, there were a bunch of Zoo-Wee Mamas in there that we never handed in to the school paper.

Greg said I should put them in here because they were gonna be worth a lot of money when he gets famous.

I told Greg maybe we should write some MORE Zoo-Wee Mamas but he said that joke is stale and we need to come up with something NEW.

And then Greg had an AWESOME idea. He said we should create our own SUPERHERO. Well I liked that idea a lot because it sounded FUN. But Greg said that he didn't care about having fun, he just cared about the MONEY.

Greg said that if you come up with a superhero then you can sell the movie rights and sit back and wait for the money to roll in.

Then we started talking about what we'd do with all the money we were gonna make from our superhero idea. I said I'd go to the toy aisle at the store and I'd fill up a shopping trolley with as many toys as I could fit.

But Greg said I wasn't thinking BIG enough. He said he'd buy the whole STORE and wear a different pair of sneakers every day and he'd live in the snacks aisle.

Then I said I'd buy a fancy sports car and I'd give Ms Beck a ride to school every morning.

Greg said we were gonna be so rich we could buy the whole SCHOOL and fire all the teachers and have epic paintball fights in the hallways.

I said maybe we shouldn't fire ALL the teachers because Ms Beck is really nice and she's good at teaching maths.

Greg said we'd be so rich we wouldn't NEED to learn maths any more but we could keep Ms Beck around because we'd need someone to count our money for us. And I guess that made me feel a little better.

Greg said we had PLENTY of time to figure out what we were gonna do with all our money LATER ON but right now it was time to get serious about this superhero idea.

Greg said the FIRST thing we needed to do was figure out what kind of POWERS our superhero should have.

I said maybe he could fly or have super strength but Greg said both those ideas were dumb because they've been done a million times before.

Then I said maybe our superhero could have X-ray vision but Greg said that wasn't a good superpower because once he accidentally saw his grandpa naked and he wishes he HADN'T.

Greg said we needed to do something ORIGINAL so we started coming up with ideas that no one had ever THOUGHT of before. And the ideas we came up with were OK but not great.

The one we liked the best was this guy called the Chuckster who could throw his own HEAD like a football.

But Greg said the Chuckster wouldn't work as an action figure because the head would be a choking hazard for little kids.

Then we tried to come up with some characters that WOULD be OK if a kid accidentally swallowed them but most of our ideas weren't that good.

CHEESE STICK BOY

CHICKEN FINGER LADY

Greg said moms are usually the ones who buy their kids toys so we should come up with something THEY'D like. But we weren't happy with that idea either.

Greg said maybe the reason we weren't coming up with anything good was that we weren't a very good TEAM. He said we should each try working on our OWN and see who could come up with a better idea.

We both did our own thing and then we showed each other our work.

Greg's superhero was a guy from space who had a different kind of power in each fingertip which was actually a pretty awesome idea.

I told Greg his idea was cool and we should go with THAT.

Then Greg said well what's YOUR idea? But I didn't wanna tell him because I knew he'd laugh. And then he promised he WOULDN'T laugh so I showed him my character.

Greg asked what Amazing Guy's superpower was and I said it was KINDNESS. And that made Greg break his promise about not laughing.

Greg said a superhero should be EDGY and it would be cool if Amazing Guy had knives coming out of his knuckles and wore a black leather jacket and said swears when he fights the bad guys.

But I said I wanted Amazing Guy to be a role model for children, and that made Greg break his promise a second time.

POUND
POUND

I told Greg if he didn't like my character that was fine but I wasn't giving him any money if I sold the MOVIE rights. And all of a sudden Greg got real interested in Amazing Guy and said if I get rich I owe him half the money because I used his markers and paper.

I said that wasn't true and Greg said he'd call his lawyer to find out. Then Greg dialled a number on the phone and I listened in on his half of the conversation.

MM HMM. YEP, THEY'RE MY MARKERS. FIFTY PER CENT? OK THAT'S WHAT I THOUGHT.

Then Greg hung up the phone. I told him to call his lawyer BACK because I wanted to ask him a few questions.

But Greg said I couldn't AFFORD his
lawyer and I had to get my own.

Greg said since we were gonna split things
50-50 then we were equal partners and
we needed to work TOGETHER. I said
fine but I still don't want Amazing Guy
to say swears and Greg said OK we'll talk
about that later.

Greg said the FIRST thing we needed to
do was give Amazing Guy an "origin story"
to show how he got his powers. Then he
told me how OTHER superheroes got
their powers.

I said Amazing Guy just had good parents who raised him to be a nice person and that's why he decided when he grew up he'd fight for people who needed his help.

But Greg said that's a TERRIBLE origin story. He said something EXCITING needed to happen, like Amazing Guy gets hit by a meteor or gets bitten by a radioactive bug or something like that.

And I said OK fine then Amazing Guy gets hit by a double rainbow and THAT'S how he gets his powers.

Greg said that didn't make SENSE but he didn't feel like getting into a dumb argument about rainbows so we'd come back to the origin story later on too.

Greg said every good superhero has a secret identity so we needed to come up with one for Amazing Guy.

I said he could be a nurse at an emergency care clinic and when he gets off work at 6:00 p.m. he becomes Amazing Guy and then helps people until his bedtime.

And no one knows his secret identity, not even Nurse Beck who works with him at the emergency care place.

Greg said I got that name from Ms Beck our maths teacher but I said nope it's just a coincidence.

Greg said we were wasting too much time talking about stupid stuff and we needed to design Amazing Guy's SUIT.

I said I liked the suit I came up with just FINE but Greg said it was stupid because everyone could tell who he was if they saw him walking around in regular life.

Greg said Amazing Guy needed a mask, so
he drew one that looked pretty awesome.
And he added a cape too.

Then Greg said if Amazing Guy doesn't
have any real powers then maybe his
SUIT could have powers. But I said
Amazing Guy has the power of KINDNESS
and his gloves are padded so he doesn't
hurt the bad guys too much.

I said I wanted to do all the drawings
and Greg said that's fine but he'd do the
WRITING. So I drew this awesome scene
where Amazing Guy has to leave work
early to fight some bad guys and I left
space for Greg to fill in the words.

I told Greg he totally messed up my comic and that from now on I'd do the drawing AND the writing. Then Greg said he was gonna call his lawyer again and I said go right AHEAD. And even when he said he was gonna call SANTA I wouldn't budge.

Greg said he didn't want to write for my stupid comic anyway because my superhero was terrible and he said he was just gonna write Intergalactic Man comics and I said fine because my character was BETTER.

Then Greg said if Intergalactic Man got in a fight with Amazing Guy he'd wipe him out in like five seconds. And I said oh yeah let's see about THAT. So then we drew this battle and he drew HIS superhero and I drew MINE.

I guess I got a little carried away with that last drawing because after I drew it Greg said it was probably time for me to go home.

Maybe next time I won't have Amazing Guy use his FULL powers on his enemies. Because I wouldn't want his parents or Nurse Beck to be disappointed in him.

THE TIME ME AND GREG HAD A TWO-NIGHT SLEEPOVER

OK you already know this from the title of the chapter, but this one time me and Greg had a TWO-NIGHT SLEEPOVER. And I bet you think we had a total blast and you want to read about all the wacky stuff we did, but guess what? It was not that fun at ALL.

The reason this sleepover happened was because my Nana got sick and me and my parents were gonna go visit her but then Mrs Heffley said:

When my mom said OK to that idea, me and Greg were HYPED because we never had a two-night sleepover before. But I guess we should've waited until later to celebrate because of the whole Nana thing.

SLAP

On Friday my mom packed my bag for the weekend and she put in an extra pair of underwear "just in case".

Plus she packed a picture of her and my dad so I could look at it if I missed them too much while they were gone.

Like I said before, the sleepover wasn't a lot of fun but it started off pretty good. We played video games in Greg's basement and ate snacks. Then we prank-called Scotty Douglas and he blew the whistle he keeps right by his phone for when we do that.

EXCUSE ME SIR YOUR REFRIGERATOR IS RUNNING SO MAYBE YOU SHOULD GO CATCH IT.

TWEET

But then Mrs Douglas called Mrs Heffley to tell on us for prank-calling Scotty. Then Mrs Heffley told us we were "bullying" and that made me feel ashamed.

At 9:00 Mrs Heffley said it was time for bed and she went back upstairs.

I was pretty tired but Greg said he had an idea. There is this kid on our street named Joseph O'Rourke who has a trampoline but he never lets anyone use it. Greg said we should sneak out and jump on the trampoline while Joe was asleep.

Well I wasn't so crazy about this sneaking-out idea but Greg said if I was going to be a baby I should go up to Manny's room and sleep in THERE.

I said I wasn't a baby and he said "Yuh-huh"
and I said "Nuh-uh." Then he said "Yuh-
huh times INFINITY" but I was ready
for that and I said "Nuh-uh times infinity
SQUARED." And I thought I had Greg beat
with that one, but he got me anyway
when he said "Yuh-huh times infinity
squared plus ONE."

So we snuck out of the back door and I
followed Greg up to Joe's. It was really
cold outside and all I had on were my
jammies, but I didn't wanna complain
because then Greg might call me a baby
again.

Sure enough all the lights at the O'Rourkes' house were off so this was our big chance to use Joe's trampoline. Greg said we couldn't make any noise and then he climbed up and did a bunch of jumps but he was real quiet.

Then it was MY turn. This was my first time on a trampoline and it was REALLY fun, and I guess that's why I forgot we were being sneaky.

172

The lights came on inside the O'Rourkes' house and their dog started barking and Greg took off without me. I wanted to run TOO but it's not so easy to stop bouncing when you're on a trampoline.

Once I finally stopped I ran to the Heffleys' house and went around to the back door.

But I guess Greg wanted to teach me a
lesson for making too much noise at the
O'Rourkes' because he wouldn't let me in.

I tried to show Greg that I was freezing
but I don't think he really got what I was
trying to tell him.

I thought he was gonna make me stay out
there all NIGHT so I ran around the house
to see if the front door was unlocked.

But it WASN'T and I kind of freaked out a little.

The good news is that someone came to the door pretty quick but the bad news is that it was Mr Heffley.

Mr Heffley told us to get our stuff from
the basement because we were gonna
have to stay in Greg's room so he could
keep an eye on us.

Then Mrs Heffley came into Greg's room
and said she was disappointed in us for
sneaking out and that made me feel
ashamed all over again. But I think Greg
gets in trouble a LOT because he didn't
seem that ashamed.

As soon as Mrs Heffley went to bed, Greg said I was dumb for making all that noise at the O'Rourkes' and EXTRA dumb for ringing the doorbell. I said I was sorry for saying "wheeee" on the trampoline but the doorbell thing was all his fault.

Then Greg whapped me with his pillow and I whapped him BACK but I guess we made too much noise and that's why I had to see Mr Heffley in his underwear for the second time in one night.

Mr Heffley told Greg he had to sleep in
Manny's room and all I could think was,
who's the baby NOW?

The next day Mrs Heffley woke me up
and said breakfast was ready downstairs.

Greg was in the bathroom brushing his
teeth and he said he hoped I brought my
own toothpaste because if I wanted to
use his I was gonna have to pay for it
since it was his house.

I told him I DID have my own toothpaste
and then he said I was gonna have to pay
for the water I used to brush my teeth.

I said I wasn't gonna pay for the water
because I was the guest and guests are
supposed to get treated SPECIAL.

So he said if I wasn't gonna pay what
I owed I couldn't eat breakfast or any
other meals either.

I was like yeah RIGHT and then he said I
was using his electricity and he shut the
light off on me.

When I got downstairs I told Mrs Heffley
about all the stuff Greg said upstairs and
she said I was RIGHT about guests being
special.

Then she let me pick which pancakes I
wanted before Greg got to pick.

After breakfast Mrs Heffley said we had
too much screen time the day before and
that we had to figure out something to
do until lunch.

Greg was in a grumpy mood so I decided
to cheer him up with a knock-knock joke.
But he wouldn't do the "who's there" part
no matter how many times I tried.

I told Greg I was gonna go upstairs and tell his mom he wasn't saying "who's there". And that finally made him do it.

I said what do elephants do at night? But Greg said you're not supposed to ask a question in that part of a knock-knock joke and I said yes you are.

Then he told me I was dumb and I said I was gonna tell on him for THAT. And Greg said go right ahead and so I DID.

So Mrs Heffley came down and told Greg
he wasn't allowed to call me dumb or
stupid or any other bad names either.

But then when she left, Greg said he had a
new nickname for me. At first I thought it
sounded cool but then I figured out what
he MEANT.

HEY STOOP.

I told Greg I was gonna tell on him AGAIN but then Greg said that it was Opposite Day and everything meant the opposite of what it was supposed to.

Well I knew what he MEANT so I went and told Mrs Heffley. But at first she didn't get mad because she didn't know it was Opposite Day.

I explained it to Mrs Heffley and she made Greg apologize. But I think he might've been being opposite.

Mrs Heffley told us that sometimes friends get on each other's nerves but we needed to figure things out since we had a whole day to go on our sleepover.

She said maybe we should spend some time apart and I thought that sounded like a GREAT idea. So I hung out with Manny in his room for a while.

Even though I was having fun with Manny, I missed my mom and dad and I looked at their picture whenever I got the chance.

WHIMPER

The next time I saw Greg was when we had lunch. Mrs Heffley made peanut butter and jam sandwiches and she even remembered to cut the crusts off mine.

After we finished our sandwiches she gave us chocolate-chip cookies for dessert. She gave Greg one but she gave me TWO because she said I was the guest and guests are SPECIAL.

I ate one of my cookies but I made a shield around the other cookie with my arms so Greg couldn't get it. Sometimes if I have something Greg wants he will lick it so I won't want it any more.

That's what he did last Halloween when I
got more candy than he did.

But Greg said he was full and didn't even
WANT my cookie. He said that while I was
playing with Manny he was reading a book
about magic and he wanted to show me a
trick. I really like magic so I said OK.

First Greg told me to put my fingers on
the edge of the table so they were close
together like this:

Then Greg took my glass of milk and put it on top of my fingers.

I asked him when the magic part was gonna happen and he said it was ALREADY happening because I couldn't move. Well he was right because if I did, the glass of milk would tip over and spill. And Mr Heffley gets mad when I spill stuff in his house.

But then Greg said here's the REAL magic part and he took my cookie and ate it up.

GOBBLE
GOBBLE

After that, Greg went upstairs but I was stuck at the kitchen table. And I was still there a half hour later when Mrs Heffley came back to the kitchen.

I told her what Greg did and boy was she mad but it wasn't because of the magic trick. She was mad that Greg took something that belonged to me without asking.

We went up to Greg's room and then
Mrs Heffley told me I could pick out one
of Greg's things to take home with me so
we'd be even.

Well Greg had a BUNCH of cool toys that
he never let me play with so it was really
hard to pick. But every time I got close
to one of his favourites he kind of let me
know I shouldn't pick that one.

I picked an action figure that was a knight with a missing arm and Greg seemed OK with that.

But as soon as Mrs Heffley left the room Greg said I could play with my lame action figure because he was gonna play with all his cool stuff by himself.

It kind of bugged me and I wanted to bug Greg BACK. So I pretended I was having a total blast with my toy.

TRA LA LA LA LA I'M HAVING SO MUCH FUN. TRA LA LA LA LA!

Well it WORKED and Greg said I had to hand over his toy. I said no way and he said he was just gonna wait for me to fall asleep and he'd take it back HIMSELF.

I told him I was gonna put the action figure down my underwear so he couldn't get it and he didn't like that idea.

Then Greg said he'd TRADE me for the action figure and I asked him what he'd give me for it. Greg said he'd give me ninety-nine cents for the knight and I said OK to that.

But then Greg took a dirty sock out of his hamper and tried to get me to smell it.

And I was like what was that for? And Greg said that was my first "scent".

I said I wanted ninety-nine CENTS not ninety-nine SCENTS. But Greg said a deal's a deal and then he tried to get me to smell another sock as my second scent.

When I told Greg I was gonna go tell on him again, he said he'd trade me his Lego dragon for my knight and I said YES because that dragon is way better than a knight with no arm.

But then when I gave Greg my knight he wouldn't give me the dragon because he said I should've remembered it was still Opposite Day.

Well that was the last straw for me and I tried to grab the dragon from Greg. But it kind of slipped out of my hands and hit the floor and broke apart.

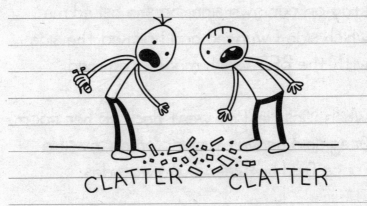

CLATTER   CLATTER

I guess we were making a lot of noise because the next thing we knew Greg's mom was back in the room. She said she was gonna have to separate us for the rest of the night which was fine with ME.

Mrs Heffley said that we each had one half of the bedroom and that we had to stay on our own side. So she asked me which side I wanted and I picked the side with the BED which made Greg mad.

When Mrs Heffley went back to her room, Greg said he was turning on an invisible force field between our two sides.

Then he said if someone crossed over they'd get zapped.

Greg said he was fine with me having the bed because he could sleep on an air mattress and plus all the fun stuff was on HIS side of the room. And when I reached over to Greg's side for my action figure, sure enough I got zapped.

ZAP!

I opened the drawer in the table next to Greg's bed to see if he had any comics I could read. Well there weren't any comics but one of Greg's old handheld video games was in there.

So I played it and Greg couldn't do anything because of the force field.

But Greg said I could play video games by myself like a nerd because he was having a wild party on HIS side of the room and I wasn't invited. And I got kind of jealous because his party looked pretty fun.

I said well I'm having a party on MY
side and it was even more wild than HIS
party and I had really good music. Greg
said I couldn't even come up with an
original idea but I still think he was jealous
of my party.

Then Greg said the plug to my party speakers was on HIS side of the room so he pulled it out to shut off my music.

Greg got back to his party and I tried to tell him to plug my speakers back in but Greg couldn't hear me because the music at his party was too loud.

But this time MR Heffley came into the room and Greg didn't notice him standing in the doorway.

Mr Heffley said he didn't want one more peep out of us and then he left the room. We were both quiet for a long time but then Greg tried to get me to laugh and I almost did.

I was kind of glad we had to be quiet
because I was getting pretty sleepy
anyway and I wanted to go to bed.

I told Greg I needed to brush my teeth
and he said too bad because the force
field was still on and I was trapped in my
half of the room for the whole night.

So I asked if he could just turn off the
force field for a little while so I could brush
my teeth but he said once the force field
is turned on it stays on until the morning.

And then Greg went to the bathroom to
brush HIS teeth and came back to the
room after he was done.

That's when I remembered I need to use the bathroom before I go to bed every night so I don't have any accidents.

But Greg said I was just gonna have to hold it until the morning. I said I couldn't MAKE it all the way to morning and Greg said that wasn't his problem.

I said if Greg didn't shut off the force field I was gonna have to pee into the Chewbacca mug on the table next to Greg's bed. Then he told me he had a special invisible knife that could cut through the force field.

Greg showed me how the knife worked by cutting a square in the force field right next to the table where the mug was.

Then he reached through the hole and grabbed the mug.

I asked Greg to cut a Rowley-sized hole in the force field so I could get through it to use the bathroom.

But Greg said the knife ran on invisible
batteries and they got used up when he
made HIS hole so I was out of luck.

Then Greg started talking about all sorts
of things that made me feel like I really
needed to use the bathroom.

Finally Greg got tired and he fell asleep. I
thought about trying to sneak past him
but I was worried he was just faking it
and I was gonna get zapped.

After a while I fell asleep too. But I woke up around six in the morning feeling like I was gonna BURST.

I didn't care about the force field any more but I was worried that if I used the bathroom I might wake up Mr Heffley. But I should've just used the bathroom anyway because Mr Heffley was already up for the day.

SPLISH!

Luckily Mr Heffley didn't look up in time to see me at the window and when he got to Greg's room I was already back in bed.

I fell back asleep after a while and got up when Mrs Heffley said it was time for breakfast.

After we ate, I went to get my knight action figure from Greg's room but I couldn't find the toy ANYWHERE.

Greg said he didn't know what happened to it, but Mrs Heffley said he had to help me look for it.

So the two of us searched Greg's room
but to be honest he wasn't all that helpful.

I guess Mrs Heffley thought Greg was
hiding the action figure from me because
she said if he didn't hand it over in two
minutes then he was gonna be in big
trouble.

Greg said he needed to use the bathroom
but he'd keep looking for my action figure
after he was done. But I noticed he had
something in his hand when he went in
there.

Greg locked the bathroom door and Mrs Heffley told him to come out right this instant. But then the toilet flushed and when Greg opened the door there wasn't anything in his hand any more.

Mrs Heffley made Greg give me THREE toys and this time I picked out ones that WEREN'T broken.

My mom and dad came and got me just before lunch and boy was I glad to see them. And P.S. if you wanted to know the answer to that knock-knock joke, it's "Elephants watch elevision."

THE ADVENTURES OF
GREG AND ROWLEY

I'm pretty much up to date on Greg's life so today I showed Greg what I wrote so far. I thought he would like it but he was MAD.

Greg said this book was supposed to be about HIM and not about ME. I told him it was hard to write about just HIM because most of the time we do stuff TOGETHER.

He said I need to go back through the book and take out all the stuff with me in it. I told him that would be dumb because then the book would only be like one page long.

I said maybe we should change the title to "THE ADVENTURES OF GREG AND ROWLEY" and it could be OUR biography.

Then I said since there's a lot of scary stuff in this book we could make it into a spooky series where these two pals solve mysteries. We could make a lot of money and we'd BOTH be rich and famous.

Greg said that was the stupidest idea he ever heard.

He said this book is about HIS life and if he wants to he can change the name of Greg's best friend to "Rupert" and then he wouldn't owe me ANYTHING. Plus he said he'd make Rupert really dumb and drooling all the time.

Then Greg told me the book smelled funny anyway and when I brought it up to my nose to sniff it he closed the book on my face.

WHAP

So I said hey what was THAT for? And Greg said that's what I got for dropping him in the puddle.

Then he said he got me back when I least expected it and I guess he was right about THAT.

But I was pretty mad and I whapped him with his own biography.

WHAP

Well I guess Greg wasn't expecting THAT because he lost his balance and fell in a big puddle.

Anyway I am up in my room now and I am hoping Greg's mom calls him home for bedtime soon because he already skipped dinner.

I'm glad all that stuff happened today because it gave me a whole new chapter in our biography. I'm sure we'll be pals again tomorrow and we'll have a bunch of new adventures that I can put in here.

And I'll bet if we go with my idea about the scary stuff it'll sell a million copies.

But if Greg changes my name to Rupert I just want to say for the record that he wet his pants at that first sleepover too.

<u>OK Now Back to This Being About Me</u>
Well if Greg's not happy with his biography
then I can go back to using this journal to
write about MYSELF.

So now I'm officially the main character
of this book again. And from now on this
thing is just gonna be about me and my
mom and my dad and I might mention
Ms Beck one more time if there's enough
room.

Speaking of my mom and dad, after my
last fight with Greg they came to my
room to talk about it.

ROWLEY MAYBE IT'S TIME TO
FIND SOME NEW FRIENDS.

But I don't really think I can add any new friends because Greg takes up so much of my time.

I know me and Greg don't always get along but like Mrs Heffley said, sometimes friends get on each other's nerves.

Well me and Greg get on each other's nerves a LOT so I guess that just proves that we're

I TOLD YOU IT WAS GONNA BE BAD!

Feeling sneaky?

Check out this **EXCLUSIVE EXTRACT** from

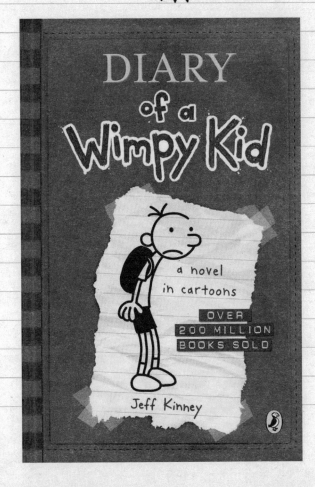

SEPTEMBER

<u>Tuesday</u>

First of all, let me get something straight: this is a JOURNAL, not a diary. I know what it says on the cover, but when Mom went out to buy this thing I SPECIFICALLY told her to get one that didn't say "diary" on it.

Great. All I need is for some jerk to catch me carrying this book around and get the wrong idea.

The other thing I want to clear up right away is that this was MOM's idea, not mine.

But if she thinks I'm going to write down my "feelings" in here or whatever, she's crazy. So just don't expect me to be all "Dear Diary" this and "Dear Diary" that.

The only reason I agreed to do this at all is because I figure later on when I'm rich and famous, I'll have better things to do than answer people's stupid questions all day long. So this book is gonna come in handy.

Like I said, I'll be famous one day, but for now I'm stuck in middle school with a bunch of morons.

Let me just say for the record that I think middle school is the dumbest idea ever invented. You've got kids like me who haven't hit their growth spurt yet mixed in with these gorillas who need to shave twice a day.

OUTTA MY WAY, RUNTS!

And then they wonder why bullying is such a big problem in middle school.

If it was up to me, grade levels would be based on height, not age. But then again, I guess that would mean kids like Chirag Gupta would still be in the first grade.

Today is the first day of school, and right now we're just waiting around for the teacher to hurry up and finish the seating chart. So I figured I might as well write in this book to pass the time.

By the way, let me give you some good advice. On the first day of school, you've got to be real careful where you sit. You walk into the classroom and just plunk your stuff down on any old desk and the next thing you know the teacher is saying —

I HOPE YOU ALL LIKE WHERE YOU'RE SITTING, BECAUSE THESE ARE YOUR PERMANENT SEATS.

GAAH!

So in this class, I got stuck with Chris Hosey in front of me and Lionel James at the back of me.

Jason Brill came in late and almost sat to my right, but luckily I stopped that from happening at the last second.

Next period, I should just sit in the middle of a bunch of hot girls as soon as I step in the room. But I guess if I do that, it just proves I didn't learn anything from last year.

Man, I don't know WHAT is up with girls these days. It used to be a whole lot simpler back in elementary school. The deal was, if you were the fastest runner in your class, you got all the girls.

And in the fifth grade, the fastest runner was Ronnie McCoy.

Nowadays, it's a whole lot more complicated. Now it's about the kind of clothes you wear or how rich you are or if you have a cute butt or whatever. And kids like Ronnie McCoy are scratching their heads wondering what the heck happened.

The most popular boy in my grade is Bryce Anderson. The thing that really stinks is that I have ALWAYS been into girls, but kids like Bryce have only come around in the last couple of years.

I remember how Bryce used to act back in elementary school.

But of course now I don't get any credit for sticking with the girls all this time.

Like I said, Bryce is the most popular kid in our grade, so that leaves all the rest of us guys scrambling for the other spots.

The best I can figure is that I'm somewhere around 52nd or 53rd most popular this year. But the good news is that I'm about to move up one spot because Charlie Davies is above me, and he's getting his braces next week.

I try to explain all this popularity stuff to my friend Rowley (who is probably hovering right around the 150 mark, by the way), but I think it just goes in one ear and out the other with him.

Wednesday

Today we had Phys Ed, so the first thing I did when I got outside was sneak off to the basketball court to see if the Cheese was still there. And sure enough, it was.

That piece of Cheese has been sitting on the court since last spring. I guess it must've dropped out of someone's sandwich or something. After a couple of days, the Cheese started getting all mouldy and nasty. Nobody would play basketball on the court where the Cheese was, even though that was the only court that had a hoop with a net.

Then one day, this kid named Darren Walsh touched the Cheese with his finger, and that's what started this thing called the Cheese Touch. It's basically like the Cooties. If you get the Cheese Touch, you're stuck with it until you pass it on to someone else.

The only way to protect yourself from the Cheese Touch is to cross your fingers.

But it's not that easy remembering to keep your fingers crossed every moment of the day. I ended up taping mine together so they'd stay crossed all the time. I got a D in handwriting, but it was totally worth it.

This one kid named Abe Hall got the Cheese Touch in April, and nobody would even come near him for the rest of the year. This summer Abe moved away to California and took the Cheese Touch with him.

I just hope someone doesn't start the Cheese Touch up again, because I don't need that kind of stress in my life any more.

Have you read them all?

THE ONE WITH THE
BIG BROTHER

THE ONE WHERE
GREG SHAPES UP

THE ONE WITH THE
CRAZY SNOW STORM

THE ONE WITH
THE VALENTINE'S
DANCE

THE ONE WHERE
GREG NEEDS
A NEW FRIEND

THE ONE WITH THE
FAMILY ROAD TRIP

THE ONE WITH THE
SCARY SCHOOL TRIP

THE ONE WHERE
GREG AND ROWLEY
MAKE A
HORROR FILM

THE ONE WITH
THE HOLIDAY
DISASTER

THE ONE WITH
THE WINTER
BATTLE

THE ONE WITH THE
HEFFLEYS' HOME
DISASTER

THE ONE THAT
ROWLEY WROTE

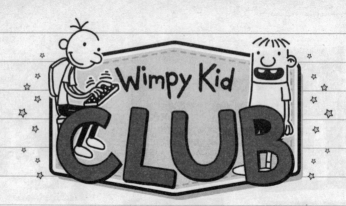

www.wimpykidclub.co.uk

- Watch TONS of cool videos

- Enter AWESOME competitions

- Take the WIMP WARS challenge!

- Read EXTRACTS from the books

- Download must-have FREEBIES!

Sign up for the newsletter to get ALL the latest **Wimpy Kid** gossip FIRST!